MW01102688

For Nick,
the silliest
samurai I
have ever met
– *Tony Flowers*

For Chloe-San, the
shōgunista, and the
three all-powerful
mini-shōguns, Adam,
Luke and Olivia
– *Nick Falk*

A Random House book
Published by Random House Australia Pty Ltd
Level 3, 100 Pacific Highway, North Sydney NSW 2060
www.randomhouse.com.au

Penguin
Random House
RANDOM HOUSE BOOKS

First published by Random House Australia in 2015

Random House Books is part of the Penguin Random House group of companies
whose addresses can be found at global.penguinrandomhouse.com

National Library of Australia
Cataloguing-in-Publication Entry

Authors: Falk, Nicholas; Flowers, Tony
Title: The race for the shōgun's treasure
ISBN: 978 0 85798 636 8 (pbk)
Series: Samurai vs ninja; 2
Target Audience: For primary school age
Subjects: Samurai – Juvenile fiction
          Ninja – Juvenile fiction
Other Authors/Contributors: Flowers, Tony
Dewey Number: A823.4

Cover and internal illustrations by Tony Flowers
Internal design by Tony Flowers
Typeset by Midland Typesetters, Australia
Printed in Australia by Griffin Press, an accredited ISO AS/NZS 14001:2004
Environmental Management System printer

Random House Australia uses papers that are natural, renewable and recyclable
products and made from wood grown in sustainable forests. The logging and
manufacturing processes are expected to conform to the environmental regulations
of the country of origin.

SAMURAI VS NINJA

THE RACE FOR THE SHŌGUN'S TREASURE

NICK FALK and TONY FLOWERS

RANDOM HOUSE AUSTRALIA

On Honshu, the largest island in Japan, is a city called Tokyo.

Three hundred years ago, Tokyo was called Edo. The streets were dark and dusty. The houses were made of paper.

It was a city of mystery and magic.

It was midnight. Somewhere in the darkness a pig snuffled. Nearby an old man picked his nose. But nobody noticed. There were no lightbulbs in Edo Period Japan.

A thief, dressed in black, raced through the city streets.

The thief wore soft-soled tabi
boots, silencing each footstep.
The thief was heading for
Edo Castle, home of
the shōgun.

The shōgun was ruler of all Japan. He was as mighty as a mountain and as powerful as a peregrine falcon. No-one dared disobey him.

No-one, except for one.

Two hulking guards stood by the castle gates. The thief pulled a bamboo straw from a secret pocket.

Two dried peas zipped through the air.

The guards collapsed to the ground.

The thief somersaulted over the guards and climbed up the castle walls, as silent as a spider.

The thief stopped, crouched down low
and listened.

The thief had come to steal the
shōgun's greatest treasure – Oguma-za
the Great Bear.

The thief had come back for revenge.

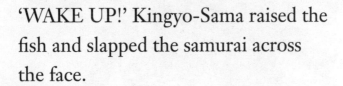

'WAKE UP!' Kingyo-Sama raised the
fish and slapped the samurai across
the face.

The samurai squawked
and tumbled from
his bed. He had
only slept for
two hours.

His head felt
like a pot
of sticky
custard.
But he
had to obey.

8

In the far north of Japan, at the peak of the Tiger's Claw, was Castle Kemushi (the hairy caterpillar). This was the home of the samurai.

Kingyo-Sama was head of the samurai. He was esteemed Master Goldfish, and here his word was law.

The samurai practised the art of Nodo no Kingyo, the Way of the Thirsty Goldfish. It was an ancient martial art, passed down from the Great Shark himself.

'A goldfish needs no sleep!' barked Kingyo-Sama, marching up the line of semi-dozing samurai.

'We must always be alert! We must always be on guard! Danger lurks around every corner!'

He raised the fish above his head. 'Let morning practice commence!'

Staggering and groaning, the samurai followed him outside.

Across the Hidden Valley, at the peak of
the Dragon's Tooth, was Castle Baka-
Tori (the idiot chicken), home of the
ninja. In the largest room of the tallest
tower, Buta-Sama opened one eye.

Buta-Sama was head of the ninja. He
liked to sleep. He was very, very good
at it. In a sleeping contest between
the greatest sleepers in the world,
Buta-Sama would have won.

Buta-Sama reached for his telescope. He balanced it on his belly and peered through the lens.

The samurai were out on the walls of Castle Kemushi, sparring with their swords. Most of them were too tired to lift their arms. Kingyo-Sama stalked amongst them, slapping shirkers with his trusty fish.

Idiotic Samurai

grumbled
Buta-Sama.

I'll send them something to REALLY wake them up.

Buta-Sama leaned
over and eyed
the poopy-pot
under his bed.
It was full. There
were no toilets
in Edo Period
Japan.

Someone was knocking on the gates of Castle Kemushi.

Kingyo-Sama smacked a snoozing samurai and sent him scurrying to see who it was.

'Whoever it is, tell them to come back after breakfast!' Kingyo-Sama barked.

But the scuttling samurai did no such thing.

He returned, red-faced, his eyes bulging.

he stammered.

Kingyo-Sama's knees wobbled.

A hatamoto. A personal guard of the shōgun himself. A warrior of ancient legend.

Kingyo-Sama could hardly breathe. His eyes were fixed upon the gate.

And he was not disappointed. Out of the shadows emerged an awesome figure. A giant in a jet-black kimono, clutching a glittering sword, riding an enormous armoured horse.

The hatamoto climbed off his horse. He stepped into the moonlight. He opened his mouth to speak and . . .

SPLAT!

It started raining ninja poo.

The hatamoto was covered from head to foot. It went in his hair, up his nose and down his silk kimono. He was not pleased. Not one bit. He growled:

Kingyo-Sama nodded, face as white as a ghost's backside.

enquired the hatamoto.

Kingyo-Sama cringed as he replied.

He waited for the hatamoto to draw his sword. He knew the punishment for pooing on a hatamoto. Death. By beheading.

'Hmm . . .' rumbled the hatamoto, wiping his sticky forehead. 'Strange weather you have in these parts.'

Kingyo-Sama was saved. Hatamoto were brave. But they weren't very clever.

The mighty warrior pulled a scroll from his sleeve. He cleared his throat.

'In the name of the shōgun, Kingyo-Sama and his samurai are called to Edo Castle. A mighty quest awaits you!'

'Me?' gasped Kingyo-Sama. 'The shōgun wants *me*?'

'Yes!' boomed the hatamoto. 'You are to leave at once!'

And with that the hatamoto departed, ignoring the poo trickling into his ear.

Kingyo-Sama's heart was pounding. *I can't believe it*, he thought. *The shōgun has called for me. Finally my moment has come!*

Kingyo-Sama closed his eyes. He smiled. This is what he imagined:

*The shōgun
will make me
Hatamoto-sama,
Lord of Goldfish.
Buta-Sama will
be forced to bow
before me.*

*I will abolish all of the ninja, kick them out
of Castle Baka Tori, and make them live in
pigsties.*

I will force them to
work in the vegetable
garden and wear
underpants on
their heads.

On weekends
I will make them
eat poo pie.

Without cream.

I will be very,
very happy.

Kingyo-Sama was fuming. Smoke was coming out of his ears. He was standing in the great hall of Edo Castle, his samurai in strict formation behind him.

Everything was perfect. Except that Buta-Sama was standing next to him, grinning from ear to ear.

Ninja in Edo Castle?
It was a disgrace!

Suddenly, a burly hatamoto boomed:

All eyes turned to the front. A teeny tiny man stepped on to the stage. He was so small his bottom was brushing the ground.

'Ninja and samurai!' he squeaked. 'I am the great and powerful shōgun, ruler of all Japan. You may now kowtow before me.'

Everyone kowtowed. A couple of ninja stifled a giggle.

'I have called you here to catch a very naughty person,' cheeped the shōgun. 'This person stole the Great Bear, Oguma-za. And I want it back at once!'

Kingyo-Sama gasped. He had heard
of Oguma-za. It was the shōgun's most
priceless possession.

'But great and powerful shōgun,'
stuttered Kingyo-Sama, 'who would
steal such a treasure?'

The shōgun opened his mouth to
answer. But before he could speak . . .

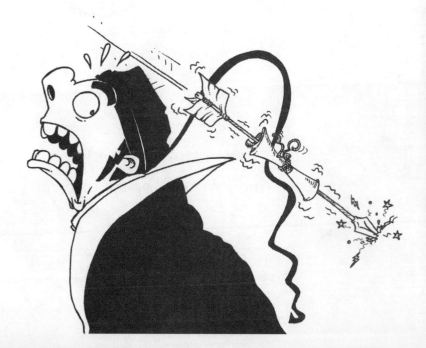

A silver arrow smashed through the
window and thwonked into the wall
behind the shōgun's head.

Mummy squealed the shōgun,
leaping into a
hatamoto's arms.

There was a note tied to the arrow. Another hatamoto stepped forward and unrolled it. The note read:

If you seek Oguma-za, come and find me in the Mystic Cave of Moshi-Moshi.
– Akira the Thief

Everyone gasped. Akira. The most dangerous thief in all of Japan. Legend has it he would kill a man just for sneezing.

Kingyo-Sama gulped. Buta-Sama scratched his bum.

'Whoever brings the Great Bear back to me,' chirruped the shōgun, 'will be made ruler of the Hidden Valley!'

Kingyo-Sama and Buta-Sama turned to look at one another. They both knew what this meant. If one of them was made ruler, the other one would be finished . . .

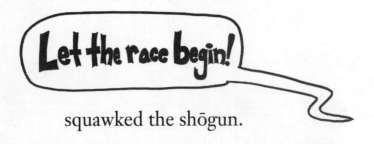

squawked the shōgun.

For a moment no-one moved. And then, in a clatter of swords and a clutter of nunchucks, the ninja and samurai raced from the room.

'Blue-bottomed banana brains!'

'Purple-panted party poopers!'

'Soggy-stockinged sushi scoffers!'

'Knobbly-nippled nincompoops!'

The ninja and samurai raced across the hilltops, insulting each other as they ran.

'You silly ninja will never reach the
Mystic Cave!' yelled Kingyo-Sama.

'The danger
of death is
too great!'

'HA!' boomed Buta-Sama. 'We ninja laugh in the face of death. Danger is our middle name!'

'Mine isn't,' squeaked a nervous ninja. 'My middle name is Sid.'

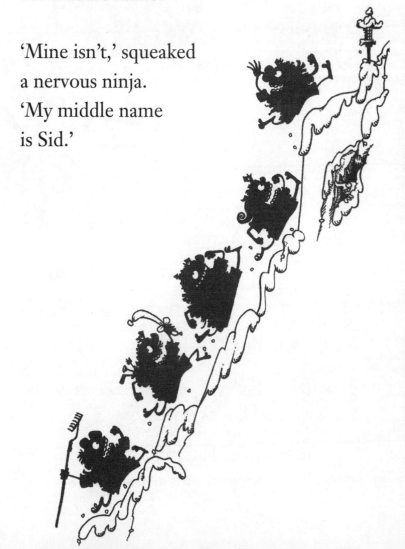

There was good
reason to be
scared. To reach
the cave, three
frightful obstacles
had to be
overcome.

The Cliffs of Zetsubou
(despair) – cliffs so steep
they scared themselves.

Ku fu (terror) Canyon – a canyon so
deep it had lost its bottom.

Fuan (fear) Forest – a forest so creepy
the trees had knock knees.

Only idiots would attempt such a crazy
quest. The shōgun had chosen well.

The samurai and ninja
reached the Cliffs of Zetsubou
at dawn. They were so tall the
tops were covered in clouds.

But Kingyo-Sama didn't blink.

'Flippers of Steel!' he barked.

The samurai lined up in rows.
They locked their elbows
and flexed their fingers.
Their arms became steel rods,
their fingers iron claws.

'Upsy daisies!'

The samurai started to climb.

'Catch ya later,
ninja whingers!'
Kingyo-Sama
shouted.

The ninja gaped. They practised the
ancient art of Mink-u-i Buta – the Way
of the Ugly Pig. It was very good for
gobbling cakes. But not so good for
climbing.

But Little Pig, the smallest ninja, had an
idea. She whispered in Buta-Sama's ear.
Buta-Sama smiled. It was
a very good idea.

'Flying Pigs of
Power!' he
commanded.

The ninja reached inside their shinobi shōzokus. They pulled out red hot chillies. Every ninja carried one. It was standard emergency equipment.

'Prepare for jet propulsion!' ordered Buta-Sama.

The ninja ate their chillies. They started to sweat. These were no ordinary chillies. They were super-extra-spicy-hot-exploding-fiery-death chillies.

'Launch positions!' commanded Buta-Sama.

The ninja spread their legs. They clenched their tummies. A grumbling rumble began to grow . . .

'FIRE!' boomed the ninja leader.

. . . their bottoms erupted.

The valley was flooded with fire.

Up and up the ninja flew, jetting past the sweaty samurai.

 screeched Kingyo-Sama.

But the ninja were ahead. They scampered away, sprinting samurai hot on their heels.

By nightfall they reached Ku fu
Canyon. It was terrible to behold.
A hundred yards across with edges
as sharp as daggers.

But Kingyo-Sama wasn't flustered.
He commanded:

The samurai shook out their arms.
They stretched and lengthened like
octopus tentacles.

 ordered
Kingyo-Sama.

The samurai lined up in twos.
Each grabbed the other by
the ankles.

screamed
Kingyo-Sama.

And fling they did. They flung and
flung until only a single flinger was left.

Beat that

jeered the final
flinger, sneering at
the snotty ninja.

Buta-Sama snorted. 'Pathetic,' he grunted.

He clapped his hands. A gigantic ninja pushed his way forwards, tummy jiggling like a jumbly jelly.

'Behold the Sumo-San.' Buta-Sama grinned.

Sumo-San clicked his heels. He bowed.
He waddled to the edge and lay down.
His stomach was so big it blocked out
the moon.

'Let the leaping commence!'

Little Pig was the first to jump. She
sprinted up to Sumo-San and hopped
onto his belly.

'WAHOO!'

Up through the sky she soared, somersaulting as she went.

'HEEYAH!'

She landed, perfectly poised, on the other side.

One by one, the ninja bounced and boinged. They leapt and leapt until only Sumo-San was left.

'Put that in your potty and munch it.' Sumo-San smiled.

Finally they reached Fuan Forest.

Terrible tales were told
of Fuan Forest. Tales of
flesh-munching
were-goats and
fifteen-fingered
vampire voles.
Tales of ghosts
and ghouls and
gobbledygooks.

But Kingyo-Sama didn't pause.

 he barked.

The shaking samurai drew their swords.

'Samurai, hold hands!'

The samurai held hands. A few
of them stuck their thumbs
in their mouths.

'Samurai, advance!'

The terrified samurai
advanced into the
woods.

Buta-Sama blinked. He didn't want to admit it, but he was scared stiff.

There was only one thing for it.

'Ninja! Remove your socks!'
he snapped.

The ninja whipped off their socks.

'Party Conga
Formation!'

The ninja formed a conga line, hands on the shoulders of the ninja in front.

'Blindfolds on!'

Each ninja tied a stinky sock around the eyes of the ninja in front. It was a plan of genius. Now they wouldn't see anything scary at all!

'FORWARD!'

The ninja conga-ed blindly into the
woods.

The samurai were soon lost. They staggered forwards, swords drawn, blinking into the blackness.

When, suddenly, they stopped.

Something was slithering towards them. A slippery, slimy snake, sliding between the trees.

'Camouflage!' whispered Kingyo-Sama.

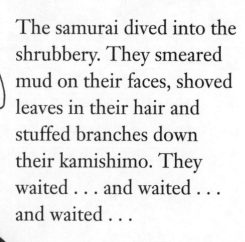

The samurai dived into the shrubbery. They smeared mud on their faces, shoved leaves in their hair and stuffed branches down their kamishimo. They waited . . . and waited . . . and waited . . .

Screaming and shrieking, they sprung their surprise.

'We're under attack!' cried the ninja.

They leapt out of the Conga
Formation, ripped off their blindfolds
and whipped out their swords.

Fearsome creatures were all around
them. Beasts with lumpy mud faces,
crinkly-leaf hair and bodies of prickles
and sticks.

A bloodcurdling battle began.

Swords slashed, shurikens
shrieked, nunchucks struck.

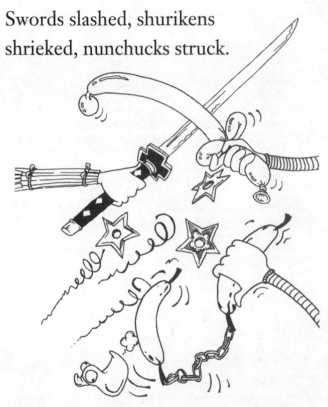

Socks were shoved up noses. Sticks
were poked in ears. And in the frenzy
of fighting, soon no-one knew who
was who or what was what or
which was which.

Until a figure
appeared in
the shadows.
A mysterious
figure in black.

'Akira!' whispered
Kingyo-Sama.

The thief turned tail and ran.
Kingyo-Sama removed his foot from
Buta-Sama's armpit and they both
barrelled after him.

Further into the forest they flew.
Until finally, in the darkest part of
the deepest gully, they found it.

The Mystic Cave of Moshi-Moshi.

Bats squeaked high above. Eyes spied
from the shadows.

Deeper and deeper into the cave
they delved. Until . . .

GASP!

There it sat. Bathed in moonlight on a pillar of stone. The most famous treasure in all of Japan.

Oguma-za.

The shōgun's favourite stuffed toy.

'It's a teddy.' Buta-Sama giggled.

'It's *my* teddy,' snarled Kingyo-Sama.

They both raced forward to claim it.

'Not so fast!'

Someone somersaulted between them.

It was Akira the Thief.

A black mask covered his face. In his
hand he held a fearsome sword.

You shall not touch this teddy

he growled.

'In the name of the shōgun, we shall,' cried Kingyo-Sama and Buta-Sama.

Buta-Sama struck first. He used the Trotters of Thundering Terror, the most deadly move he knew.

But Akira was too fast. He dodged his deadly trotters and sent Buta-Sama spinning to the ground.

Kingyo-Sama struck second. He used the Flying Fins of Fury, the most deadly move *he* knew.

But Akira was too quick. He stepped to one side and turned Kingyo-Sama topsy-turvy.

For half an hour the battle raged. Kingyo-Sama kicked, Buta-Sama flipped, but always the thief was too nimble. Until suddenly, seeing his enemies tire, Akira stopped and knelt. He held up his sword, signalling surrender.

'I am defeated,' he said.

Akira took off his mask. Long dark hair tumbled to his shoulders. Kingyo-Sama and Buta-Sama gasped.

He was not a he . . . but a she!

'The Lady Kiko,' whispered Kingyo-Sama. 'The shōgun's secret sister!'

'Yes.' Kiko nodded. 'It is I.'

'But why?' asked Buta-Sama. 'Why steal his cuddly teddy?'

'Because once it was mine,' said Kiko. 'I'd had it since I was a baby. But when my brother became shōgun, I became his slave, and my possessions became his. All I had left was my teddy. But my brother wanted it for himself. So he banished me to the Desert of Shi (death) and left me there to die.'

A single tear tumbled down her cheek.

'And now you have come to take it back to him.'

Buta-Sama and Kingyo-Sama hesitated. Finally both kowtowed.

'I cannot take this bear from you,' said Kingyo-Sama. 'The laws of Bushidō forbid it. It is against the samurai code.'

'I cannot take it either,' Buta-Sama said, yawning. 'My tummy's rumbling and I need to have a nap.'

Kiko looked up. She nodded. 'You are both honourable men. Of course, if you do not take it, my brother will dangle you by your dongles in his deepest darkest dungeon. But men as brave as you will have no fear of that.'

There was a moment's pause. A bat
scratched. A drop of water dripped.

And then Kingyo-Sama and Buta-Sama
dived for the bear.

'It's mine!'

'It's mine!'

'It's mine!'

'It's mine!'

They bit, they kicked, they poked, they flicked, they scratched, snatched, scraped and scritched. Until finally, clothing ripped and topknot twisted, Kingyo-Sama grabbed the bear and raced out of the cave.

'Noooooooo!' shrieked Buta-Sama, panting in pursuit.

Kiko watched them leave. 'Idiots,' she breathed. She had planned to lose the battle.

Soon, brother

she said, smiling,

Sweet revenge will be mine

'It's over,' Buta-Sama whimpered. 'Kingyo-Sama cannot be caught. He runs too fast. His belly is too small.'

They had been chasing the samurai for many hours. 'You must get there before him,' urged Little Pig.

'How?' wailed Buta-Sama. 'He is many miles ahead!'

Little Pig whispered in his ear. Buta-Sama grinned.

'NINJA!' he commanded. 'LEND ME YOUR UNDERPANTS!'

Kingyo-Sama staggered up the steps of Edo Castle. He crawled past the hatamoto and collapsed in front of the shōgun. 'I have brought you back Oguma-za,' he croaked.

'Yippee!' squealed the shōgun. 'My snuggle-wuggles, my cuddly-wump, my *fluffety wuffety scruff*!' He reached out to take his tiny teddy. 'Kingyo-Sama of the samurai,' he squeaked, 'I hereby make you ruler of the –'

'NOOOOO!' shouted someone high above.

Everyone looked up. There was something flying through the window. Was it a bird? Was it a plane?

No. It was Buta-Sama, pinged by a stretchy Pant-a-Pult, all the way from Ku fu Canyon.

He crashed to the ground, rolled to his feet and grabbed the bear's left leg.

'I found it too!' he cried. 'The prize belongs to me!'

'You filthy fart-breathed fool,' snarled Kingyo-Sama, tightening his grip. 'The race is over. *I* won!'

'It's not over till I say it is!' growled
Buta-Sama, tugging on the teddy.
Kingyo-Sama tugged right back.

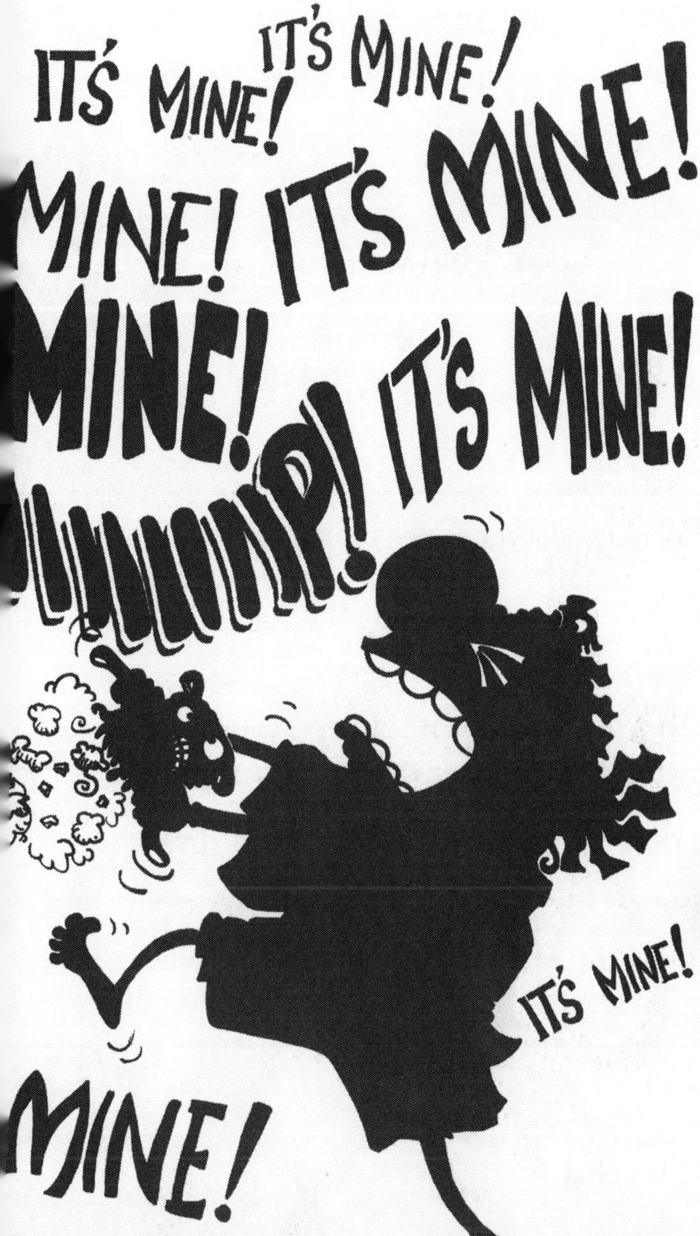

IT'S MINE!
IT'S MINE!
MINE! IT'S MINE!
MINE!
IT'S MINE!
IT'S MINE!
MINE!

Oguma-za was torn in two.

Everyone froze.

The bear's insides burst open.

It was filled with stuffing and dust
and . . .

'ITCHING POWDER!' screeched
the shōgun.

The shōgun was right. Itchy-scritchy
powder sprayed across the room. It
went up everyone's sleeves. It slid down
everyone's underpants. Eyeballs bulged,
cheeks went red. The hatamoto howled.

'Arrest them!' screamed the shōgun. 'Tie them up! Burn their bums! Tickle their tiniest toes!'

Kingyo-Sama and Buta-Sama raced from the room, a hundred hatamoto hot on their heels.

They sprinted through the city. They scampered into the hills. 'We didn't do it! It wasn't us!' they whimpered as they ran.

High on the castle battlements, a lone figure watched Kingyo-Sama and Buta-Sama run away. It was Kiko, dressed in black, a teddy tucked under her arm (the real Oguma-za).

She watched them trip each other up. She watched them fall. She watched the hatamoto dive on top of them. She smiled. Then she rose to her feet, silent as the wind, and disappeared into the night.

Deep underground,
beneath the walls of
Edo Castle, was a dark,
dank dungeon.

The walls were wet. Rats and spiders
scurried in the shadows.

It was cold and black and scary.

In the centre of the room, two dirty figures swung from side to side, dangled by their toes from the ceiling.

One was a ninja. The other was a samurai. Neither one of them looked pleased.

The samurai turned to the ninja.

'I will get you for this, brother Buta,' he croaked. 'Mark my words. One day soon, I will have my vengeance.'

Glossary

baka idiot

Bushidō samurai code of honour

buta pig

Edo Period a time in Japanese history between the years 1603 and 1868

fuan fear

hatamoto shōgun's personal guard

kamishimo a traditional outfit worn by samurai during the Edo Period

kemushi hairy caterpillar

kimono traditional Japanese dress

konnichiwa hello

ku fu terror

mink-u-i buta ugly pig

ninja a covert warrior from ancient Japan

nodo no kingyo thirsty goldfish

sama a mark of respect put after someone's name, normally used for a person of great importance

samurai Japanese warrior or knight

sayonara goodbye

shi death

shinobi shōzoku traditional ninja outfit

shōgun supreme military ruler of the Edo Period

shuriken small-bladed weapon

sumo a Japanese wrestler

zetsubou despair

Want more SAMURAI vs NINJA battles?

Check out *Samurai vs Ninja 1:*
The Battle for the Golden Egg

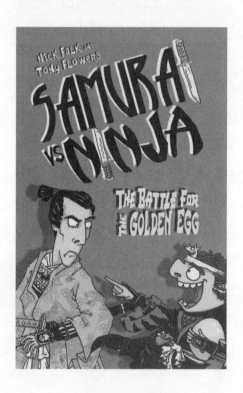

OUT NOW

Watch out for Samurai vs Ninja
books 3 and 4 in July 2015!